KATIE WOO

and Friends

by Fran Manushkin

illustrated by Tammie Lyon

capstone

Katie Woo is published by Picture Window Books
A Capstone Imprint
1710 Roe Crest Drive
North Mankato, MN 56003
www.capstonepub.com

Library of Congress Cataloging-in-Publication Data
Manushkin, Fran.
  Katie Woo and friends / by Fran Manushkin; illustrated by Tammie Lyon.
     p. cm. — (Katie Woo)
  Summary: Combines four previously published stories about Katie Woo
and her friends, including Boss of the world, The tricky tooth, Goodbye to
Goldie, and Katie goes camping.
  ISBN 978-1-4048-7909-6
  1. Woo, Katie (Fictitious character)—Juvenile fiction. 2. Friendship—Juve-
nile fiction. 3. Chinese Americans—Juvenile fiction. [1. Friendship—Fiction.
2. Chinese Americans—Fiction.] I. Lyon, Tammie. ill. II. Title. III. Series:
Manushkin, Fran. Katie Woo.
  PZ7.M3195Kbe 2012
  [E]—dc23   2012005279

Photo Credits
Fran Manushkin, pg. 96; Tammie Lyon, pg. 96

Designer: Emily Harris

Printed in the United States of America in Stevens Point, Wisconsin.
122012   007083R

Table of Contents

Boss of
the World

Katie Woo and her friends took a
trip to the beach.

"Let's do everything together!"
said Katie. "We'll have so much fun!"

"Let's build the biggest sand castle in the world!" shouted Pedro.

"You two carry the water to me.
I will build the castle," said Katie.

"That's not fun!" JoJo said.

"I think it is," replied Katie.

When the castle was finished, it wasn't very big, and it kept falling down.

"What a rotten castle!" Katie moaned.

At lunchtime, Katie shouted, "I'm so hungry, I could eat an elephant!"

"Me too!" said JoJo and Pedro.

They passed French fries around, but Katie ate most of them.

JoJo and Pedro had
only three fries each.

"I'm still hungry," said
Pedro.

Katie grinned. "I'm not!" she said.

After lunch, Katie said, "Let's lie on the blanket. We can watch the clouds and kites flying by."

"Katie, move over!" Pedro said.
"You are taking up all of the blanket!"

"It's my blanket," Katie said. She did
not move one inch. Pedro and JoJo
had to lie on the itchy sand.

"Let's go over to the playground," Pedro said. "There are big swings there."

The three friends raced each other. Katie got there first and grabbed the only empty swing.

JoJo and Pedro watched her swinging for a while. Then they walked away.

"What's wrong with them?" Katie wondered.

She ran after her
friends, saying, "Let's
look for seashells!"

The three friends
took off their shoes. They walked
barefoot along the shore. The waves
tickled their toes.

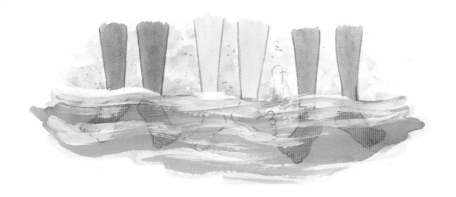

"I see a giant shell!" Pedro shouted.
He began running. But he tripped
over some driftwood and fell down.
Katie grabbed the seashell.

"Hey, that's not fair!" said JoJo.
"Pedro saw the giant shell first."

"Finders keepers," Katie insisted.

JoJo and Pedro made faces and
walked away.

Katie grabbed her beach ball and began tossing it around, but it wasn't any fun.

Just then, JoJo and Pedro and JoJo's dad began swimming and splashing around in the waves.

Katie ran over, shouting, "I want to swim too!"

"No!" yelled JoJo. "You can't! The sea belongs to us!"

"That's silly," Katie said. She laughed. "The sea can't belong to you."

"And all the French fries don't belong to you," said Pedro.

"And all the seashells," added JoJo.

"And the blankets and swings," said Pedro.

"Uh-oh!" said Katie Woo. "I think I have been a meanie."

"For sure!" said Pedro and JoJo.

"I'm sorry!" said Katie. "I won't be a meanie anymore. Is it okay if I share the sea with you?"

"Yes!" said her friends.

And there were plenty of waves for everyone!

The Tricky Tooth

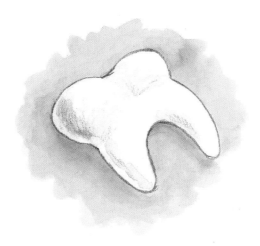

"Guess what?" Katie told JoJo. "I have a loose tooth!"

"So do I," said JoJo. "If we wiggle them, they might come out."

Katie wiggled her tooth back and forth.

So did JoJo.

"No luck," said JoJo.

"No luck," sighed Katie.

"Let's eat a lot of popcorn," said Katie. "That will make our teeth come out."

The two of them chewed and chewed. JoJo's tooth fell out!

But Katie's stayed put.

At bedtime, Katie brushed her tooth
a lot, but it didn't fall out.

"No tooth for the Tooth Fairy," Katie
sighed.

The next day, Miss Winkle asked
Katie's class, "Who has lost a tooth?"
Everyone raised their hands.
Everyone but Katie.

After school, Katie played soccer. She told Pedro, "I'll hit the ball with my head. That will make my tooth come out!"

"I love the space between my teeth," Pedro said. "It helps me whistle really loud!"

Katie sighed. "I want a space, too."

When the ball came to Katie, she
bumped it hard. She scored a goal!
But her tooth did not budge.

The next day, Katie
lost a sock, a button,
and her pencil.

But she did not lose
her tooth.

Katie's mom said, "Don't worry.
Your tooth will come out when it's
ready."

"I'm ready now!" said Katie.

Katie went to dance class. She jumped and spun around. She got very dizzy, but her tooth didn't move.

At school, Miss Winkle made a tooth chart. "Put a check on it for each tooth you have lost," she said.

Katie had no checks.

At home, Katie told her dad, "I'd like to be a blue whale. They don't have any teeth to worry about."

"That's not a good idea," teased her dad. "Our bathtub isn't big enough."

Katie's mom told Katie, "It's a mystery how teeth come out."

"It sure is," Katie groaned. "This tooth is tricky!"

The phone rang. It was Pedro. He asked Katie, "When can you come to see my new puppy?"

"Right now!" said Katie. "That will cheer me up!"

Pedro's puppy was adorable! "His name is Toto," said Pedro.

"Like in *The Wizard of Oz*," said Katie. "Cool!"

"Can I hold Toto?" Katie asked.

"Sure!" Pedro nodded. "Just be gentle."

Toto was so warm and soft, Katie nuzzled him with her cheek.

"Arf!" The puppy barked and
nuzzled Katie back.

"Hey," said Katie, "I feel something
on my tongue."

"It's my tooth!" Katie yelled. "Way to go, Toto!"

"Way to go, Katie!" said Pedro. "Now you have a space, too."

Katie couldn't stop smiling!

That night, Katie put the tooth under her pillow.

"Don't fall out or anything," she said. "I want the Tooth Fairy to find you."

And the Tooth Fairy did.

Goodbye to Goldie

Katie Woo's dog, Goldie, was very old.

One day, Goldie
became very sick. A
week later, she died.

Katie's mom held
Katie while she
cried.

"I will miss Goldie so much," Katie cried. "She was my best friend."

Katie's friend JoJo hugged her. "I will miss Goldie too," said JoJo. "She was the nicest dog in the world."

"She was!" agreed Pedro.

"Goldie loved running on the beach," said Pedro.

"We didn't have to go into the sea to get wet," said JoJo. "Goldie would just shake her fur and make us all wet!"

"Goldie was great in the snow, too!"
said Pedro. "We used to toss snowballs,
and she would try to catch them in her
mouth."

"Tell me some more happy stories about Goldie," said Katie.

JoJo grinned. "That's easy! There are so many."

"At Thanksgiving, Goldie ate my drumstick," JoJo said. "I turned around, and it was gone!"

"Goldie was smart," said Katie. "And fast!"

"Goldie was so much fun on Halloween," said Katie. "Remember the time she wore a skunk costume? She ran around and scared all the other dogs!"

"Goldie loved tickling my face with her tail," said JoJo.

"She dusted the table with it too," joked Katie's mom.

"And my computer!" added Katie's dad.

"Her tail hardly ever stopped wagging," said Katie.

"Goldie and I were both scared of thunder," said Katie. "But when we hugged, we both felt better."

"Goldie was a good cuddler," agreed Katie's mom.

Katie's dad showed her a photo. It was taken when she and Goldie were little. They were eating hot dogs together.

"This photo is great," Katie said. "I love looking at it."

JoJo had an idea. "We should make Katie a Goldie scrapbook. She can look at it whenever she feels sad."

Katie's mom found two photos of Goldie and Katie. In one, they were playing catch with a ball.

In the other, they were both very small. They were taking a nap on the grass.

Katie drew a picture of Goldie
catching popcorn in her mouth.

"She was good at that!" Katie said,
smiling. "She never missed!"

"Goldie could jump rope too," said JoJo. "And kick a soccer ball!"

"And almost catch squirrels!" added Pedro.

Chasing Squirrels

"Goldie lived a long and happy life,"
said Katie's mom.

"She sure did," said Katie.

That night at bedtime, Katie held Goldie's picture and kissed it good night.

"Goldie, I will always remember you," Katie promised.

And she always did.

Katie Goes Camping

Katie was going camping.

"I know all about camping," she told Pedro and JoJo. "It's so much fun!"

Soon they reached the woods. "First, we put up our tent," said Katie.

"Watch out!" said JoJo. "It's falling down."

"I can fix it," said Pedro.

"Way to go!" said JoJo.

"Now, let's explore!" Katie said.
"I will show you the pond."

"The pond is the other way." JoJo
pointed.

"No, it's not!" insisted Katie.

Katie ran down the path, but soon she was alone. No Pedro! No JoJo! No pond!

"I am not scared," Katie said.

She climbed a rock and looked around. She saw JoJo and Pedro coming.

"Boo!" Katie yelled.

JoJo jumped. "Katie, you scared me!"

"I'm very wild!" Katie bragged.

"It's raining," Pedro said.

Soon the rain stopped, and the sun came out.

"Look!" Katie pointed. "There's a rainbow! Let's make wishes on it."

Later, Katie's dad made a campfire, and they cooked hot dogs and marshmallows.

"Camping is tasty!" said JoJo.

Soon it was dark.
Stars filled the sky, and
fireflies filled the grass.

"I'd like to glow at
night," joked Katie.

"Me too!" said Pedro.
"Then I'd never get lost."

"I know a ghost story," said Katie's dad. "Once upon a time, there was a bloody finger."

"Stop!" yelled JoJo. "That's scary."

When they were in their tent, Pedro asked, "Are there bears around here?"

"I hope not!" said JoJo.

"I hope we see one," said Katie.

Soon Pedro and JoJo fell asleep, but Katie did not.

She was thirsty, so she tiptoed out of the tent.

Then Pedro woke up.

He was thirsty too, so he tiptoed out
of the tent.

Then JoJo woke up.

"Where is everyone?" she said.

"I don't want to be alone."

She tiptoed out of the tent.

It was very dark.

"Oh no!" said Katie. "I see a bear —
with antlers."

Katie began running.

Pedro saw something dark. "It's a ghost!" he yelled.

Pedro began running!

JoJo turned on her flashlight.

"I don't see a ghost!" She laughed.

"I see Katie and Pedro chasing each

other!"

"I wasn't scared," Katie insisted.

"And I wasn't!" said Pedro.

"Oh sure." JoJo laughed.

Back in the tent, JoJo asked Pedro and Katie, "What did you wish on the rainbow?"

"I wished I could see a ghost," said Pedro.

"You did," said Katie. "Almost!"

"I wished to go camping again," said JoJo.

"That's an easy wish to get!" Katie smiled.

"I wished I was a better camper," Katie said.

"You are a great camper!" Pedro laughed. "You are so much fun!"

"My dog likes camping with you too," said JoJo.

"Arf!" JoJo's dog agreed.

Then all the campers fell asleep.

Having Fun with Katie Woo!

Super Scrapbook Page

Lots of people love to make scrapbooks. It is fun to decorate paper with photos and other special things. The best part is you end up with a book filled with your memories. It's easy to make your own scrapbook page. Here's how:

1. Gather your supplies

First you need a piece of paper. Any type of paper will work, but if you want your page to last forever, ask an adult for acid-free paper. Other supplies include:

- crayons
- markers
- glue stick
- photos
- stickers
- anything else you want to decorate your page

2. Choose a theme

What will your page be about? A grandparent, favorite book, or vacation all make fun themes.

3. Get to work

Choose which photos you want to include. Do you want to include captions to describe your photos? What about stickers? Before you glue anything down, lay your items on your page to see how they fit. Then glue them down.

Want to make a Katie Woo scrapbook about your pet?
Download ours at capstonekids.com/characters/Katie-Woo

Toothy Treats

The best treats are ones that make you smile . . .
or in this case, ones that actually *are* smiles. Apples,
peanut butter, and marshmallows come together to
make a yummy, "toothy" treat. Before your start,
wash your hands and ask a grown-up for help.

Ingredients:

- an apple
- peanut butter
- about 40 mini marshmallows

Other things you need:

- cutting board
- apple slicer
- paring knife
- butter knife

*Makes eight mouths

What you do:

1. Setting the apple down on the cutting board, use the apple slicer to cut the apple into eight equal slices.

2. Take each slice of apple, and cut it in half. You now have 16 pieces.

3. Spread one side of an apple slice with peanut butter. Place four to five marshmallows on top of the peanut butter.

4. Spread peanut butter on a second slice of apple. Place the peanut-butter side down on top of the marshmallows. Now you have a toothy grin!

Repeat until you have used all your apple slices. This is a tasty treat that is healthy, too!

About the Author

Fran Manushkin is the author of many popular picture books, including *How Mama Brought the Spring; Baby, Come Out!; Latkes and Applesauce: A Hanukkah Story;* and *The Tushy Book*. There is a real Katie Woo — she's Fran's great-niece — but she never gets in half the trouble of the Katie Woo in the books. Fran writes on her beloved Mac computer in New York City, without the help of her two naughty cats, Miss Chippie and Goldy.

About the Illustrator

Tammie Lyon began her love for drawing at a young age while sitting at the kitchen table with her dad. She continued her love of art and eventually attended the Columbus College of Art and Design, where she earned a bachelors degree in fine art. After a brief career as a professional ballet dancer, she decided to devote herself full time to illustration. Today she lives with her husband, Lee, in Cincinnati, Ohio. Her dogs, Gus and Dudley, keep her company as she works in her studio.